A VASE

OF VERSES

Ayo Ayeni

© **Ayo Ayeni, 2023**

Published by

Hot Coffee Publishing

London.

www.hotcoffeebooks.com

info@hotcoffeebooks.com

All rights reserved. No part of this book may be reproduced, adapted, stored in a retrieval system or transmitted by any means, electronic, mechanical, photocopying, or otherwise without the prior written permission of the author.

The rights of Ayo Ayeni to be identified as the author of this work have been asserted in accordance with the Copyright, Designs and Patents Act 1988.

All visual art illustrations in this collection are commissioned works created by Ai-sha 'The Deep' Greenfield and all the rights in the works have been licenced in perpetuity to the author for unlimited use. Each piece of work in 'A Vase of Verses' is an impressionist and free line illustration in digital art. A rare combination of styles to achieve the artistic genius rendered in the works.

Dedication:

To my dearest Moyo, Oba, and Fiore,
You are the light that guides my words and the love that fuels my creativity.

To my beloved brother Deji,
You were my first and most cherished audience, always listening to my poems with unwavering support.

To my dear mother,
You provided me with the time, space, and nurturing environment to let my words flow.

To my dear father,
You introduced me to the right books early by keeping a rich library.

To 100 Club, Ese, Sammy 'The Sage' and Dapo
You helped interpret my poems and undammed my creative flow.

To The Guild of Artistes and Poets (GAP) and its founders, Audu and Paul,
Your constructive criticisms shaped my craft and enriched my journey.

With heartfelt gratitude,
Ayo Ayeni

Table of Contents

Dedication: III
I Red Roses 1
   1. BEAUTY, MY BLACK MAGIC (THE GREAT SAFARI) 2
   2. CARIBBEAN DAYS AND NIGHTS 6
   3. TO MOYO (WHEN SHE SAID YES!) 8
   4. 365 DAYS: AN ODE TO MY WIFE (ON OUR FIRST ANNIVERSARY) 9
   5. TEMPLE OF THE GROOM 13
II Purple Hyacinths 16
   6. SEASONS OF LONELINESS 17
   7. SLEEPWALKER 19
   8. DIARY OF A SLAVE 22
   9. A TRIBE CALLED SECRETS 26
   10. WICKED WITCH OF THE WILD WEST! 30
   11. SHAME 33
III Lotus 35
   12. PRINCE OF PEACE 36
   13. THE TOURIST AND THE PILGRIM 38
   14. APPLES OF GOLD *(INSPIRED BY PROVERBS 25:11)* 41
   15. SYN-TONYMS (Synonyms of Antonyms) 46
   16. MADNESS 47
   17. MIRAGE! 50

IV Chrysanthemums 52
    18.   AUGUST 31, 1997: A REQUIEM FOR PRINCESS DIANA.. 53
    19.   MEDUSA'S LOVE-CHILD 56
    20.   BLACK MONDAY: REQUIEM FOR JERRY 60
    21.   THE POINT.. 64
    22. AN ODE TO MY FATHER.. 67

I
Red Roses

Red roses gleaming bright,
Silken petals alight,
Blushing beauty invokes
Passion's tender strokes,
Hearts entwined sweetly sing,
Feel cupid take wing.

1.
BEAUTY, MY BLACK MAGIC
(THE GREAT SAFARI)

Your passion, the panacea to the forlornness of my soul

Your charm, pure as the whiteness of your dentition

Promises the gargantuan virtues of your heart

Your dark skin is as mystical as the blackness of your mysteries

Your enigma surrounds me

Like water surrounds the Seychelles.

Beauty, my Black Magic

Let the rhythm of the incantations

Of our eternal promises

Flow on like the rivers

Of the Benue and the Niger

To meet at the oneness

Of the spiritual central intercourse

Of Lokoja…

And in union flow down

To the black sanctuary of the sea-bed;

Our heart-shaped foam of infinitum.

In the loneliness of the hot, brown
Endless sands of the Great Sahara,
The uninterrupted panorama of the sun
Romancing myriad sands
And giving off hazy heat of fantastic mirage
Blurring the horizon
Till the Saharan sunsets;
For that is when the masculine handsomeness
Of the sun is sweetest to behold!
the sun has jilted its lover at the peak of ecstasy
And given way to the coldness of the invading moon.

I shall not leave you cold like the heartless sun…
I shall take you to the zenith of the Kilimanjaro
And to the very depth of the Great Rift Valley of the Tanzanian Range,
Peculiar black romance
Heightened from the Suez Canal
To the Cape of Good Hope,
And the breadth of the Cape Verde
To the Ethiopian Highlands.

Beauty, My Black Magic!
In our matrimonial safari
I shall brand you with the black stripes;
The colour of creation itself
Like the listless zebras of the Marsabit
I shall decorate your skin
With the proud colours of the
African Rainbow
Like the ornate feathers of the proud peacock
And you shall flaunt your colours
At the drooling tourist in search of Edenic beauty.

We shall ride the great rump of the bloated elephant
On Mashonaland
And dismount in the secret recesses
Of the abandoned furnaces of the Matopos
To break the evil assagais
That stab the heart
And pierce the ebony passion!

And in the nirvana of the hunch-back continent
Where we have found black peace
We shall embrace the power of Passion

That surrounds us

In this haven of Black Paradise…

Forever.

2.
CARIBBEAN DAYS AND NIGHTS

The coconut trees…

The cool ocean breeze…

Slapping through the islands

And slashing through myriad sands,

Tidal waves that wash away sorrows,

Loud calypso tunes auspices of happier tomorrows.

Swimming trunks, Bikinis

Blue waters, clean beaches,

Promises a pint of paradise,

A get-away from city sites,

Sunglasses, wide-brim hats, cold drink in hands,

Sea-smell, eau-de-cologne, ah! The smell of white sands!

The sunsets on the western horizon

And the azure sea glows as a young moon is born

Welcome to sweet Caribbean nights

Says the neon signs and dim yellow lights.

Lovers do their nightly prank

The fragrance of blue sweat; the firmaments' aphrodisiac.

Outdoors too, the waves kiss the beaches
With dawdling, gentle and lazy smooches;
The horny moon casting silver phosphorescence
Upon the libidinal sea's quintessence,
Shimmering in tranquil ecstasy…
Ah! A typical Caribbean night fantasy!

3.
TO MOYO
(WHEN SHE SAID YES!)

Occasions such as these acquire meaning
Not only in the earth but in the heavenlies,
Your intimate agreement now convening
Our families, for we are now engaged.
Our Union will unite two universes,
Reaching back and forward into time,
Eliciting new verses
Needed to accommodate the rhyme.

Our destinies, now one destiny, will now unfold,
Giving to our future generations
Our united DNA.

May we find in love a public beauty,
Equal to our private sense of duty,
No less a part of happiness than pleasure,
May bliss and passion sing to us,
And rapture be our leisure forever.
Amen

4.
365 DAYS: AN ODE TO MY WIFE (ON OUR FIRST ANNIVERSARY)

365 days...

365 ways...

Of saying 'I love you'.

Through our blissful kisses

And life's stressful hisses,

Through acerbic altercations

and romantic resolutions;

I am convinced 365 times over

that a man alone is a man forlorn,

And, hey, bachelors,

a man alone is not only a man not married,

But also one not married to his own.

I could be alive for 365 years

And would never have lived,

If I didn't live with you;

I could trudge 365 billion miles

and still would not have left,
 If I didn't leave with you;
If I went rib shopping
And tried on 6 billion rib sizes,
And we didn't size each other up,
I would stay asleep in Eden;
Never to awake..
Locked up in an unbespoke rib cage.

365 bright days
365 sun rays
365 colours of diverse loves;
One year!
Oh yeah!
Once, I was half the man that I am now...
Now I am no longer the man that I used to be
But the man I was breathed into being.

Know ye all Earth!
I found my wife
I found my life;
I have seized my fates
I have sealed my faith..

With my finger..

I wear the band..

Still on the band...

Wagon to the destination of our destiny.

Moyosoreoluwa mi,

Remember...

365 days ago...

...when we danced to Lara George's 'Ko Le Baje' ('It's Spoil-Proof')

When we danced before God, the priest

and all and sundry;

Let that music filter through the speakers of our synchronised heartbeats,

Let it be our song of the year and for all time..

and let it deafen us to all the noise that the sound studios of living could drum into our ears.

I love you ...Oh Yes! I DO!

Always and forever.

Bon Annivasaire Moyo Ayeni,

Bon Annivasaire

Abake mi.

5.
TEMPLE OF THE GROOM

It was the most magnificent thing I ever saw!

Pure gold, wick trimmers,

Sprinkling bowls, dishes and censers,

And the gold doors of the Temple…

Alas! My soul, bless Hiram!

I trembled…

The outer doors to the hallowed inner chamber

And the doors of the main hall

Shone like the sun under the fires of Mithras!

I entered the Hall;

The porch was guarded by lofty Pillars,

The beauty made me wet with torrents of blissful tears.

As the Sacred Curtains tore apart

Exposing the awesome sight of the Holy Place;

Magnificent, resplendent and splendid!

My tears of pure joy and wonder flowed freely

As this holy place transfigured me into divinity

With frozen warmth!

This was the place of worship;

The Holiest of Holies: that Sacred space!

Now that I was inside,

It looked and felt like heaven!

I rode on the tender wings of Cherub to the world

Where unborn babies flew past me in joyful play,

Until the eternal moment came!

I watched in ecstasy as the holy oil

Poured forth unto the holy altar…

A divine anointment it was!

II
Purple Hyacinths

Petals of purple, ethereal,

Awash in dusk's dimming light.

Adrift the soul in shadows dwell,

Questioning paths obscured from sight.

Lonely longing clutches tight,

Deep the darkness shrouds from below.

6.
SEASONS OF LONELINESS

Harmatan, the cold dry wind

That blows my soul's ridges,

The dry leaves of the withered tree of your love

Falls upon the lonely cracked earth of our garden

We are covered in brown dust; the colour of desolation,

The hay of forgetfulness enshrouds my mind,

The debris of memories

Ploughing through dry weeds of love,

My heart is now a mere shadow of its being

Where, through this misery, is our vegetation?

Raindrops, teardrops

Make the soil of my soul fertile

Where the seeds of loneliness

You have sown in my heart

Blossom in lush green stagnation

The plants yield their crops

To melancholy's thrill

Where the thorns choke the shoots of happiness,

The rodents, pests and parasites feed fat

Until the ghosts arrive to reap their harvest of green damnation.

7.
SLEEPWALKER

Yes, we journeyed the same way,
But you went through it in a dream,
I stared the ugly-faced reality in the eye.
We passed through marshes of misery together
You waded through in subconscious surreality
I wallowed through and drowned in it
In hard-backed reality,
When it bit
I did cry
You didn't!
For you didn't feel the pain,
You were dreaming.

My eyes were open
As we passed through dark tunnels
I saw the beast and his cohorts
You didn't!
Your eyes were closed.
You bruised your toes

As you were torn by thorns;
You didn't cry out
For you didn't feel the pains;
You were dreaming, dreaming!
I bruised mine
I cried out
For I felt the pain,
I was open-eyed conscious!

We came from the same place
We had the same destination
You slept through the journey
But I.. I lived through it!

8.
DIARY OF A SLAVE

CUBA, 1758, JONES PLANTATION

I put ma pen on pepa agin dis nite

Since is th' worst I can do than to fite

I have lernt to put ma thots to pepa

In the whiteman way since Holy Sepulka,

Jason, God rest his soul in peace,

The good Cuban who taught me this great art

Now lies beneath the seas,

Dead from his own gunshot;

If I had no reesin of some sort

To live for, I too would have been rot

Dinner for a milion crocodiles

Would have been me, but I take dem vice,

I take dem all cos o you

O Kuratu

Woe betide dat day, dat black Sabbath

Wen dem whiteman seprated us, dey put us apart,

But even the distance of big seas
Bilions of miles tho it seems
Cannot seprate our hearts, our souls, our spirits
O Kuratu, I've been torn in bits
For a thousand weeks
Ave been maimed with rods and stiks
With stings bitterer than venom
Ave lost ma left arm wen I tried to run
O Kuratu
I tried to run to you
A wuld a tred on water
To get to you and to my blackland and to your tapioca.

Dem call we all animals
Who've lost our tails
If animal is beautiful as you
Animal is wat we be Kuratu
Pray I wont die on this strange land 'fore I see you.
'ope you still ave curves like our juju hill?
I live on reminiscences, 'ope you too will?
I sleep in chains now with stub for arm
But I still dream of you and me on our calm
Greatland, as free as birds

Running hand in hand through forests and glades

And laughing with so much joy dat we cry

Only to awake in chains from where I lie

Swimming in the pool (my bed) which I wept-filled

The sharp edges of ma chain making me bleed.

Today I harvest a thousand suga cane

Under the hot sun and in heavy rain

Kuratu, I tired, I go to bed

My wooden arm ache me sore, now I drop ma pen today

But tomorrow about your memories I'll have something to still say

I will meet my brothas and sistas agin

I will meet you agin, lets hav children

On this earthly farce

No! not beyond the skies

Only this earth the blackman is villain,

Our love endures so's not in vain

I shall be wit you agin my lover,

We talk it all over

I pray God have pity on we black man

For we this earth is now bedlam

Keep your heart still

For I know its God's will

If this will end, then wen?

Ah! Kuratu, I drop ma pen.

9.
A TRIBE CALLED SECRETS

From the top of the hill

I glimpsed upon the town

Where the sun seldom shined;

No lanterns burned from windows,

No crackle of fire flames,

No whistle of night winds,

No faint gossips of rustling leaves,

No laughter of insects,

Not even yet the surreptitious slither of black cats.

Graveyard silence

Where the luxury of ghostly mourning

Would be reassuring,

Even the flowing rivers refused to share their murmurings

With the curious green grasses.

When I saw the tribesmen,

I shook with fear;

They all had no mouths!

And they moved so silently

That even one treading foot

Kept its sound a secret from the other,

On such a good evening

You wouldn't even dare to tell someone else;

To say 'good evening'

Was a closely-guarded secret.

Each tribesman had a barn

Where he stored his secrets;

The man with the biggest barn was king.

Their strange houses had neither doors or windows

But little secret traps on the roofs,

Everywhere was shut and sealed.

They even called no names here

For even your name was your secret.

They stared strangely at me

As I tip-toed through the town in silence,

They knew I wasn't one of them

For I had a mouth.

I hurried through in terror

Until I reached the town's exit

Where the gatemen
Who made sure no word exits
Roughly seized me and forcefully
Sliced off my mouth!
As I wept in terrible agony
One of them passed me a secret
 With his eye;
'You never leave Secret Town
With your mouth still in place!'

10.

WICKED WITCH OF THE WILD WEST!

Wicked Witch of the Wild West,

She emerged from the dark heart of the horizon

Balanced upon the big, black stallion; Misfortune,

Covered with the brown Saddle of Sadness.

Her Stetson hat of disguise hiding her long hair and bloody eyes,

She rides through our lush Prairies of Life,

Fording the deep Rivers of our Destinies,

Her .45 Colt of fortified, falsified Promises

Shooting random bullets of Fears and Doubts

Into our Fields of Dreams,

And is she a fast gun too!

She rides right through the fragile Forts of our Self-protective Posse,

Straight into the heart of our Counties of Life

With unfeminine gallant effrontery!

She swings into our Salons of Laughter,

Drinks all our whiskey and kisses our cowboys!

In the middle of the night

While the county folks still sleep

She creeps through our fields and harvests all our Dreams,

She gathers all our Dairy Cows of Hope,

Hangs 'em high and shoots 'em up!

With the clatter of Misfortune's hooves

Drumming in tune with our lamentations at dawn

When we finally awake,

She beats a fast retreat with our Crops of Dreams,

Back into the dark heart of the horizon from where she'd emerged…

Woe rider!

You Wicked Witch of the Wild, Wild West!

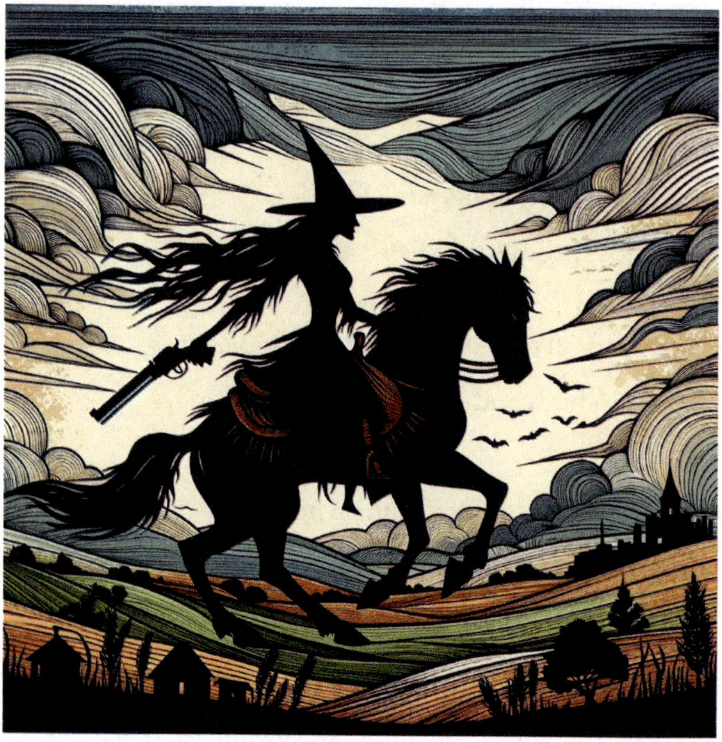

11.

SHAME

I hid my shame in the frozen moon

But the sun came at dawn

And melted the ice away

And left my shame exposed

To the light of day,

It was rotten with reproach

And stank of the faeces of demons…

…my demons.

Darkness is a traitor

It snitches on you

At the mildest interrogation of light.

Never tell the night what the volley of your voice

Cannot echo in the day

Never hide in the depth of the night

What the day cannot behold

For the beam of the sun

Shreds every tissue of the dark away

And its heat will surely thaw the frozen moon

Away into the firmament

And leave all the shame

You have hidden inside it

Exposed to the curious light of day.

It's a shame that shame cannot be hidden.

III

Lotus

Petals open with the dawn,
Harbingers of hopes reborn.
Rising up through murky deeps,
Each new day it's blessing reaps.
Promise held within its grasp,
Joy and luck contained there vast.

12.
PRINCE OF PEACE

The sweet breeze of bliss

That blows from Your trees of peace

Cause my series of miseries to cease

The soft kiss of your peace puts me at ease

And gives surcease to my soul's diseases

My melancholies find release

As my sad memories

Are trashed in the debris of histories.

The Palestinians and Israelis know this:

That peace on paper

Like pieces of paper

Can with ease be torn to pieces.

Only Your peace truly frees

I have the Prince of Peace

And now alive, I rest in peace!

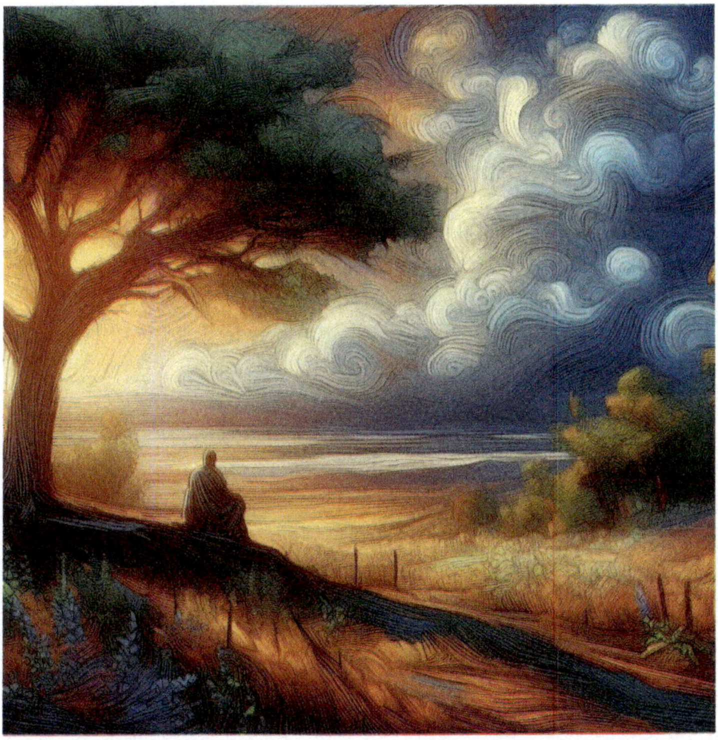

13.
THE TOURIST AND THE PILGRIM

Two strangers met on a flight and the following conversation ensued:

Tourist: Is this your first visit to the land?

Pilgrim: Yes, you?

Tourist: Same here.

Pilgrim: You just want to go sightseeing?

Tourist: Yeah, see some sights, take some photographs and all, isn't that the purpose of your visit too?

Pilgrim: No. I'm a pilgrim.

Tourist: Pilgrim, tourist, knock religion out and they're all sightseers.

Pilgrim: Tourists live by sight, pilgrims live by faith.

Tourist: Now you`re getting all religious on me. Why then do you find it necessary to go to the land? If faith knocks sight out, why didn't you just chill back home and draw on the spiritual experience of the land....by faith?

Pilgrim: I am not going to see to believe, i'm going

to see because I believe, to feel what I believe.

Tourist: The keyword is 'see'.

Pilgrim: If i was blind i'll still be a pilgrim, but who ever heard of blind sightseeing.

Tourist: I guess we live by sight.

Pilgrim: You see with your eyes, we see with our hearts, history matters to you, eternity matters to Me. For me it's the insight the sites have given me. You want to sightsee to increase your experience, I want to see sites to increase my faith. You want to see the wonders of men and nature; I want to enrich my belief in the supernatural at work in men and nature.

Tourist: Its profoundly funny how two people could walk the same land and do the same things but for absolutely different reasons and have different experiences.

Pilgrim: It's the story of mankind, we are either tourists or pilgrims here on earth.

-End-

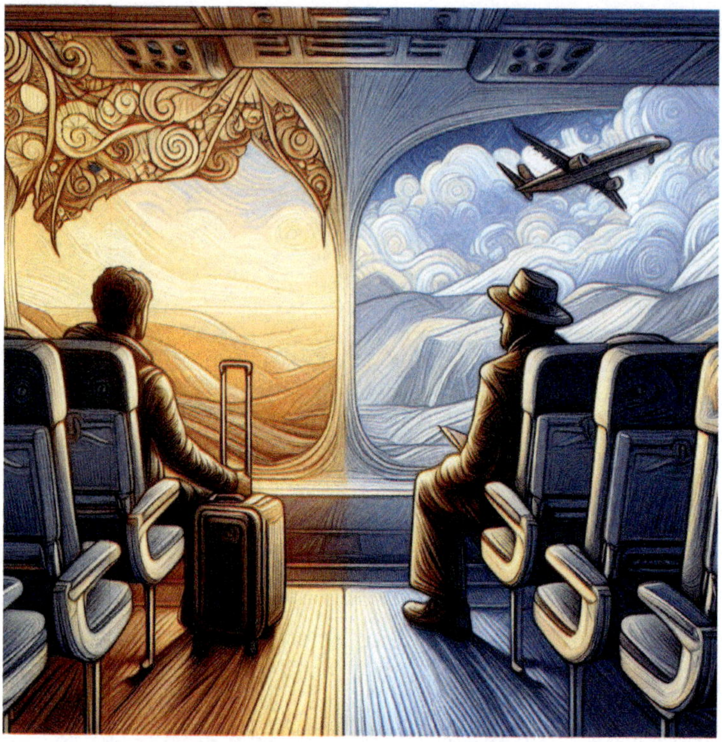

14.
APPLES OF GOLD (INSPIRED BY PROVERBS 25:11)

A word fitly spoken is like apples of gold
In settings of silver so fine, so bold
Like Wisdom's gems that shine
Epochs and eras they define
In verses elegantly proclaimed
Upon walls of time to be framed
As precious fruits of insight
Moulded flawless so bright.

"I have a dream" said Martin Luther King's voice so clear,
1963, March on Washington, we hear.
Racial equality, his vision so bright,
For a nation's future, he'd fight the fight.

"All's well that ends well," Shakespeare's muse,
In his plays, this wisdom he'd use.
Life's trials and triumphs, a journey's test,
In these renowned words, our souls find rest.

The bard's insight, an enduring chain,
Through ages, its truth will sustain.

Winston Churchill, in the face of despair,
"We shall never surrender," his steadfast prayer.
1940, Britain's darkest hour, he spoke,
Rallying the nation, in unity, they awoke.
Defiance and pride, their spirits renewed,
In those resolute words, their strength pursued.

Voltaire, in 1906, did wisely proclaim it,
"I disapprove of what you say, but I will defend to the death your right to say it."
Free speech, an ideal, democracy's creed,
In his words, a principle we all need.
To defend diverse voices, we must hold dear,
In the marketplace of ideas, let them appear.

John Donne's wisdom, from 1623's page,
"No man is an island," a timeless sage.
Interconnected, in life's vast sea we sail,
Together we rise, together we prevail.
In unity, strength, our bonds ever strong,
Through generations, his message lives on.

Franklin D. Roosevelt, in the Great Depression era,

"The only thing we have to fear is...fear itself."

He addressed, igniting hope's fire.

In 1933, with courage he led,

Restoring optimism, dispelling dread.

A nation's resilience, its spirit's revival,

In those words, a nation's survival.

Dylan Thomas, in 1933, contemplates divine power,

"The force that through the green fuse drives the flower."

He described a force within, driving flowers to bloom,

In nature's rhythm, dispelling gloom.

Life's eternal energy, an ageless theme,

In his verses, it's a vivid, living dream.

John F. Kennedy's call to inspire,

"Ask not what your country can do for you –

ask what you can do for your country." His words filled with fire.

A challenge so bold,

For country's sake, let our stories be told.

Service, sacrifice, our civic duty's demand,

In his words, a nation took a stand.

"It always seems impossible until it's done."
Said Nelson Mandela, in '94, after the victory's won.
Apartheid's end, blooming freedom's flowers.
His legacy of hope, a beacon so bright,
In his words, a world sees the light.

A word fitly spoken is like apples of gold
In settings of silver so fine, so bold
Like Wisdom's gems that shine
Epochs and eras they define
In verses elegantly proclaimed
Upon walls of time to be framed
As precious fruits of insight
Moulded flawless so bright.

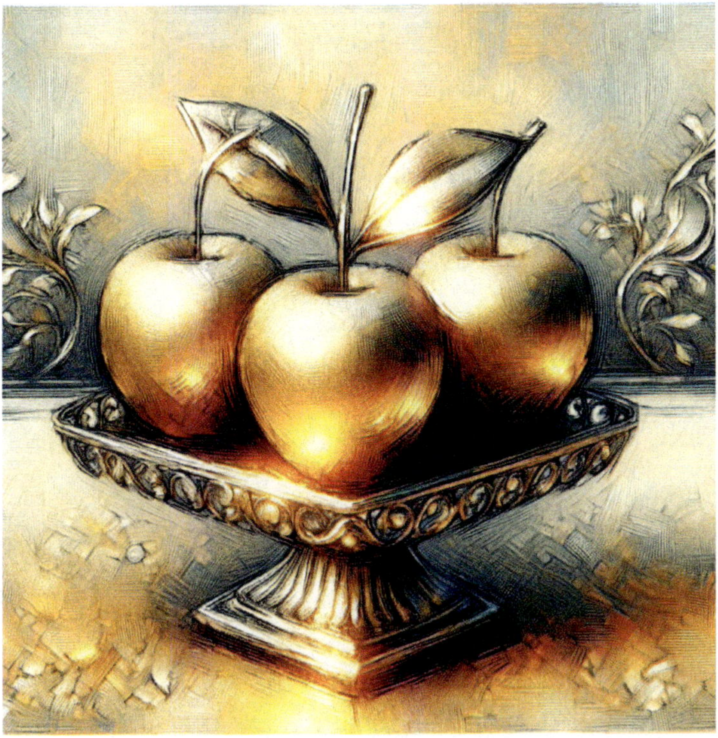

15.

SYN-TONYMS

(Synonyms of Antonyms)

Wealth is more than stacks of cash,

Joy differs from simple laughs.

No tour equals a pilgrim's path,

A house is not a homestead.

Aid only is not charity per se,

Wisdom surpasses philosophy.

Love reaches deeper than romance,

Facts betray the truth's nuance.

No wedding vows guarantee the heart,

Liberty is beyond freedom's part,

A valuable art's price tag may miss values' art.

The riches of the soul outweigh gold,

What lasts can't be bought or sold.

16.
MADNESS

The madness of my heart haunts the moon

Now the moon shines lunacy upon the world

And the darkness of its light

Is far too dim to illuminate the sparkle of wisdom.

The oceans leap in maddening storms

To tango with sister moon,

It is always night in the hearts of madmen.

Shadows have come alive

To subject their objects

To their own shadows,

Illusions have been projected

Into our own dimension;

We have, thus, become animated

And our fantasies have escaped out of our minds

To imprison us in theirs

We have worked for the fulfilment of our dreams

And have now walked into them

We now dream of basic realities
Too fantastic to be achieved
Truth now dwells in the ancient city of Myths
And its inhabitants are its depopulated believers.

But now we see, darkly
A ray of light that shines in a dark place
Until the day dawns
And the morning star rises in our hearts
Then shall the madness be cast away
With the darkness
For when the light shines
Darkness cannot comprehend it
The moon has ruled the night
Now the sun will rule the day
And shine sanity upon the world again.

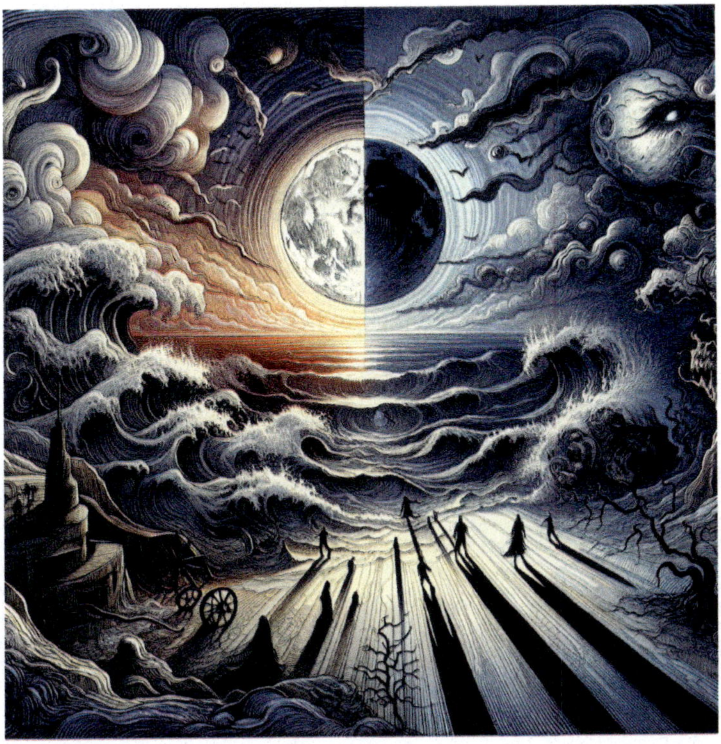

17.

MIRAGE!

The tropical scourge of the sun

Heartless, scorching, makes me burn

I know death lurks in this desert sands

I drown in liquid fantasies on thirsty lands

Oh! If only for a droplet…

I will live to see the sunset

Desert hopes, I am trying…

Maybe it's a prayer for the dying.

The mourning sounds of silence

The admirable vulture's diligence

Time is the space between them and supper

Darkness closes in on me, thicker…deeper…

I lay down to stop the misty hallucinations,

I dream I am floating upon deserts of oceans,

I dream the sand storming waves carry me to silent lands

Where famished waters dine on fiery sands.

As darkness falls, an oasis emerges

With sparkling pools and sweet date palms

I drink the waters, nourishment surges

In dawn's glow, salvation's balm

The desert trials now behind,

I'm borne on wings of fortune's gale

With fiery sands and birds left behind

Toward shores where destiny sets sail.

IV
Chrysanthemums

Flowers of golden sorrow,

Hearts break on the morrow.

Depths of grief unfold,

When loved ones of old,

Pass to shadows afar.

O sorrowing star.

18.
AUGUST 31, 1997: A REQUIEM FOR PRINCESS DIANA

In the neon-lit Place del' Alma tunnel

They crept…they waited…

They were the very best: professionals

Camera-slingers, gun-slingers

Paparazzi, assassins

Same difference

They have never missed a shot on target

In their entire career

This was not their first job

Of course, not their last.

Their instructions were simple:

Load! Shoot! Vamoose!

They crept…they waited…

Soon the Mercedes Benz 600

Would sweep by

And the cameras, guns

Would be out of their slinging holsters

And…triggered!
Soon the shots of the paparazzi, assassins
Must pierce and still the heart of England's Rose
They had waited long for this night,
This was the big one
Tonight, the princess must die!
Still, they crept, they waited
Patiently…

Looking through the zoom lenses
Of their lethal weapons
Each hoping to catch the first shot.
They grinned in the silent darkness
Of the tunnel…
Then the car's headlights pierced
The darkness of the tunnel…

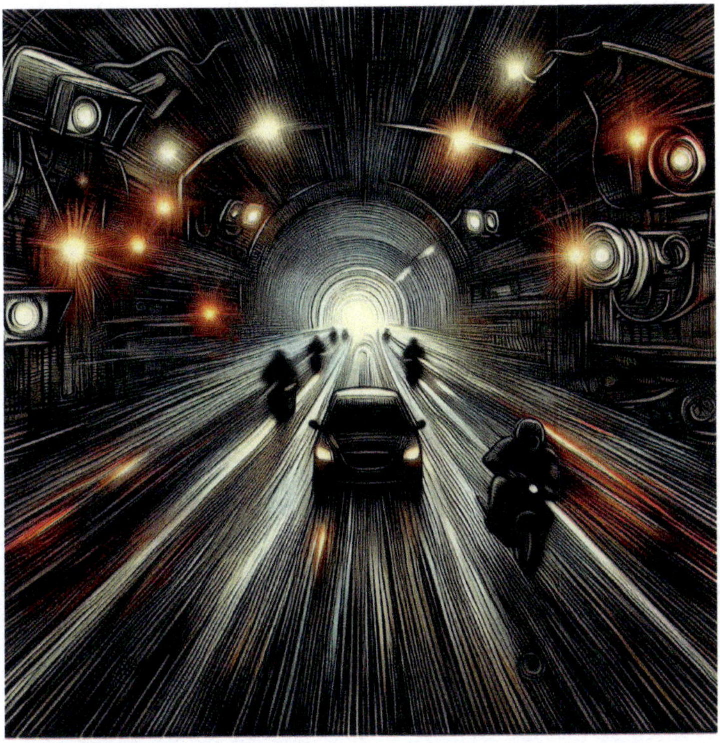

19.
MEDUSA'S LOVE-CHILD

The fragrance of Versace's birth is blown
In Zephyr's breath.
The child, the heir to the throne of Hermes;
Clad in the apparel of the gods
Reflected in the rainbow's fluorescent eyes,
Wrapped in a piece of Madonna's veil,
He is lifted from the maternity to the couturier's table,
A pair of golden scissors and a tailor's tape
Were festooned around his umbilical cord,
An immeasurable length of fashionable genius:
Medusa's love child is born.

Suddenly he has the globe in his eyes...
Then in his hands,
The subtle intricacy of gossamer threads
On his fingertips.

Through the lonely seamstress' cottage of Milan
To the palatial mansions of Lake Como;

The serpentine dirge from the flute

Sing a song of sadness;

It tells of the aurora of Versus,

The marble wealth of Istante,

The flora of Dreamers,

The celebrations of Mainlines and V2's,

The kaleidoscopic colours that

Carried in the air the perfumes

Of Red and Blue Jeans, Black and White

And several jeans.

The pageant of Juno-esque models,

The banquet of angelisque mannequins

Donning the raiment of the gods…

…But the sad serenade of the Fife's tune

Could not appease the appointed vagrant soul

Of Cunanan's bullets;

Propelled by euphoric lunacy disguised in romantic ecstasy,

He would not sit still till the bidding is done.

The volley of the shots re-echoed

The ricocheting tune of a pacifying mother

Just as the chronometer chimed dawn!

A peacock from the Café
Saw the colourful flame
That once illuminated the Cosmo,
A dove on the Piazza saw his soul
Fly past on nightingale's wings
Clad in the garments of the gods
To claim the mythic crown of Hermes.

The torrent of titanic tears
Splatters upon myriad jeans and velvet,
It floods the snake pits of Medusa's hair.
Medusa's tears flooded the seas
As she scatters his cremated ashes
Upon the earth's pillars:
Her face, a memoriam,
The logo on everything her son,
Versace ever touched.
1997.
For Gianni Versace

(Being my entry for the annual edition of the international Sozopol Fiction & Poetry Seminars (1998), organised by the Elizabeth Kostova Foundation)

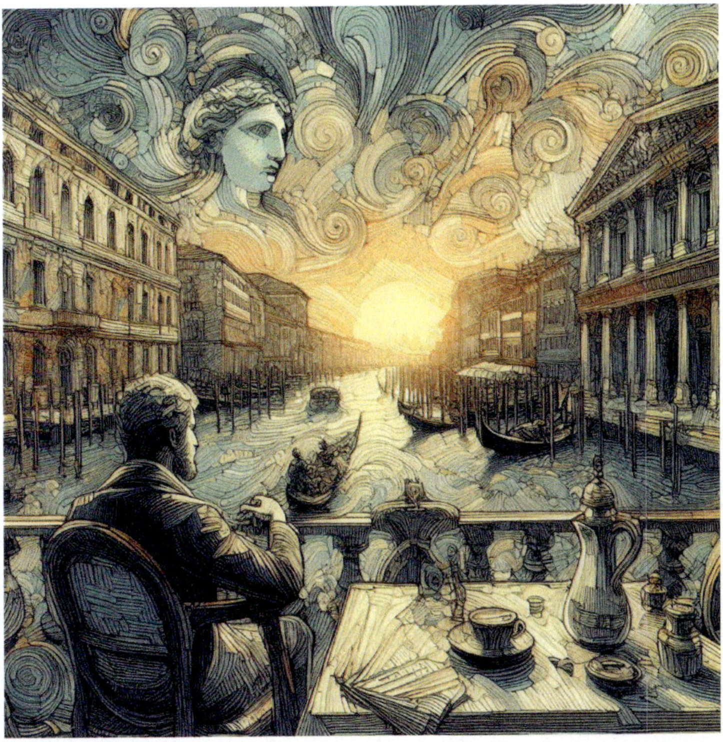

20.
BLACK MONDAY: REQUIEM FOR JERRY

Today…yes…. tonight

The fires fade and dumps ashes in its place

Darkness enters in a triumphal trumpet's blare

As it watches the retreating

Light fading into oblivion

Behind the blurry horizon.

The Eastern moon shone on

The blood-soaked sword

Searching for infidel heads

In exchange for seventy virgins in paradise.

God is life…

But you murdered life in the name of God!

Live! Live!

My soul screams sore

Why you of all the statistics to make?

My ear drums beat in hardcore rhythm

To the stampeding desperation
In tune with your baritone heartbeat,
When you screamed in Stephonic martyrdom
Waiting for the eastern moon
To eclipse upon the light of the Shining Sun.

I hear your blood cells wondering
Why kill life to have life?
I see your face amidst the stokes
But your voice is swallowed up in the eastern wind
Your handsomeness mangled by the darkness of
Moon rays on shining swords.

I watch you through rivers of tears
That wash the verdure of the earth away
To dump its debris at your feet.
Can this half lunar-tic, blood-horny moon
Rape the sun out of your life?
No! Jerry! No!
It can only touch your fleshy cloak
But your soul is hidden in Christ with God.

The angels carry you far…far away

From Black Monday
And every other day on this dark earth
Into the presence of
The Prince of Peace
Where you rest in peace.

Jeremiah Alaiyedeno
Was killed by islamic fanatics on
Black Monday (Nov. 2002)
During the Kaduna religious riots.

R.I.P

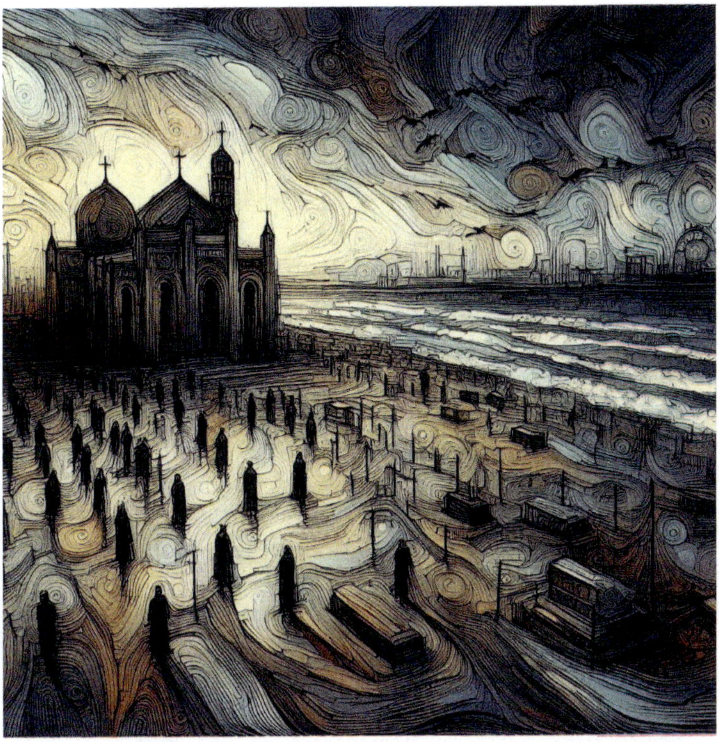

21.

THE POINT

I first saw you sitting by the bar in the pub of life,

We clicked artfully as our glasses clinked delightfully…

A few beers and many bubbles of laughter later

We knew we had to work on several sitcoms and stage plays together;

I only had to mention that sitcom idea I still hadn't scripted beyond its synopsis…

You already had a most creative montage for it!

You big, fat genius!!

That was our first night…

Our last night was no different…

I saw you…again… by the bar at The Dome…

There was no whiff of doom in the air…

Only the whiff of smoke from several cigarettes

Burning from several lungs in the dimly-lit lounge,

How could I have known it was symbolic

Of the vivid metaphors of our puffed-up and snuffed-out lives…

Snuffed to ashes…

In ashtrays…Our coffins!

I should have known it then…

After all, it was a British American Tobacco event!

A few hugs and many bubbles of beer and laughter later…

We parted to meet again… when next I visit Abuja…

Or so we thought.

You said to Tokunboh, who last saw you alive:

"I'm off to The Point."

He thought you meant that earthly location called 'The Point'…

The fancy Abuja club where life is danced away.

Little did he know you meant 'THE POINT…OF NO RETURN.'

A pointed question now confronts us all at this point of death;

"WHAT IS THE POINT OF THIS LIFE?"

(28-5-06)

For Dapo Kaizer who died in a car crash in the early hours of the 26th of May 2006

(Rest In Peace till we rendezvous at The Point where we'll live to die no more)

22.

AN ODE TO MY FATHER

My father - sturdy oak of a man,

Strong shoulders carrying life's weight in stride,

Bearing up the frail, shielding clan and stranger-

Tireless steward for all seeking refuge.

His partnership with Mother so endearing,

United front of mirth in lockstep dress.

Amidst stern mores they refused conformity,

Blazing trail for love's bold tenderness.

He gave of pockets, larders, time and hearth

So all who knocked might rest from sorrow's chase.

With him, no cry for help met deafened ears
Compassion's warm embrace bestowing grace.

No day so dark that banished Father's signature laughter

Contagious chorus soon set worries skittering!

Robust guffaws alone could counter grief.

What strength he drew from joy's deep wellspring!

The bookman, formally a book seller as a young man,

Built rich libraries for our young hungry minds,

Filled with works from the likes of

James Joyce, Obafemi Awolowo,

Ernest Hemmingway, Samuel Ajayi Crowther and Sigmund Freud.

Kindled our fires of insight with King James bible,

Tuned our hearts with hymns from Sacred Songs and Solos,

Played the harmonica, the tambourine and the shekere –

Awakening thoughts in song and verse that shape futures,

Turned children to seekers on Wisdom's stage.

Engineer and pastor

A tool in the hands of God

Called to shepherd lost sheep back to the fold,

He buried doubts beneath Faith's sturdy roots.

Many found through his care Heaven's garden –

Sanctuary blooming eternal fruits.

Stalwart oak now falls to Time's axe-strokes –

But oh the seeds his shade nurtured sprout yet!

His laugh echoes on in hearts swelling with new life –

The Pastor's legacy of love we can never forget.

RIP Dad

David Ige Ayeni

1st May 1941 - 24th Sept, 2018

A Vase of Verses is a poignant collection of poetry that delves into the depths of human experience, emotion, and imagination. Each poem in this collection is like a unique flower, collectively arranged in a vase of diverse themes and styles. The verses range from introspective musings to vivid narratives, creating a tapestry of thoughts and feelings that resonate with the soul. This compilation is an ode to the beauty of words and their power to evoke, inspire, and heal. It's a treasure trove for lovers of poetry and those who seek to explore the intricate landscapes of the heart and mind.

There are 22 poems in this collection.

About the Poet: Ayo Ayeni is a member of the Guild of Artists and Poets (The GAP) which began in Abuja, Nigeria. He lives in London, with his wife and two children.